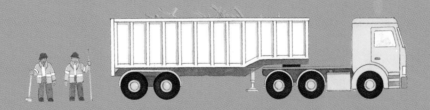

For Mum, who gave me stories, and Dad, who gave me music. SS

For Sher. BL

First published 2012
by Walker Books Ltd
87 Vauxhall Walk, London SE11 5HJ

This edition published 2014

10 9 8 7 6 5 4 3

Text © 2012 Sally Sutton
Illustrations © 2012 Brian Lovelock

The right of Sally Sutton and Brian Lovelock to be identified as author
and illustrator respectively of this work has been asserted by them
in accordance with the Copyright, Designs and Patents Act 1988

This book has been typeset in Franklin Gothic Extra Condensed

Printed in China

British Library Cataloguing in Publication Data:
a catalogue record for this book is available
from the British Library

ISBN 978-1-4063-3881-2

www.walker.co.uk

DEMOLITION

SALLY SUTTON · ILLUSTRATED BY BRIAN LOVELOCK

WALKER BOOKS
AND SUBSIDIARIES

LONDON • BOSTON • SYDNEY • AUCKLAND

Grab your gear. Grab your gear.

Buckle, tie and strap.

Safety jackets, boots and hats.

Zip! STAMP!
SNAP!

Swing the ball. Swing the ball.

Thump and smash and whack.

Bring the top floors tumbling down.

Bang! CLANG! CRACK!

Work the jaws. Work the jaws.

Bite and tear and slash.

Dinosaurs had teeth like this!

Rip! ROAR!

CRASH!

Ram the walls. Ram the walls.

Bash and smash and slam.

First they wobble, then they fall.

Thud! CREAK!
WHAM!

Hose the dust. Hose the dust.

Dampen down the dirt.

Careful, now! Don't cough or choke!

Whish! SPLISH! SQUIRT!

Crush the stone. Crush the stone.
Chip and grind and munch.
Make new concrete
from the old.

Whirr! CHURR! CRUNCH!

Shred the wood. Shred the wood.

Split and chop and chip.

Turn the sawdust into mulch.

Sort the steel. Sort the steel.
Heave and toss and bang.
Metal can be used again.

Clink! CLANK! CLANG!

Load the trucks. Load the trucks.

Lift and shift and heap.

Drive away the piles of junk.

Whump! WHOP! BEEP!

Build the hut. Build the hut.

Tap and twist and knock.

Don't forget the monkey bars!

Join the fun. Join the fun.

Run and climb and play.

Give three cheers! The job is done.

Hip... hip...

HOORaY!

MACHINE FACTS

TRUCK: A truck takes material off the site.

WRECKING BALL: This heavy steel ball is hung from a crane and swung into the side of the building to smash it.

BULLDOZER: This bulldozer has a thick steel rake for ramming walls.

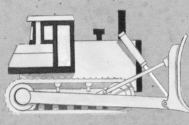

WOOD CHIPPER: A wood chipper shreds wood into sawdust, which can then be used as mulch for gardens.

HIGH-REACH EXCAVATOR: This excavator has a long boom arm which can reach a tall building to pull it down.

MOBILE CRUSHER: A crusher grinds up broken concrete which can be used to help make new concrete. This crusher can be moved.

ROTATIONAL HYDRAULIC SHEARS: Rotational hydraulic shears can be attached to excavators to cut through concrete, steel or wood.

Sally Sutton is the author of the award-winning *Roadworks* and *Demolition*, and also enjoys writing plays. She lives in Auckland, New Zealand, with her husband and two daughters.

Brian Lovelock is a scientist who has painted all his life. He has travelled widely and gained much inspiration from other cultures. Brian lives in Auckland, New Zealand, with his partner and two children.

Also by Sally Sutton and Brian Lovelock:

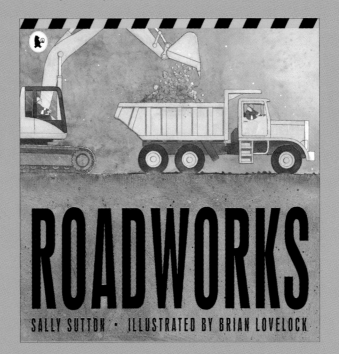

ISBN 978-1-4063-2537-9

Available from all good booksellers

www.walker.co.uk